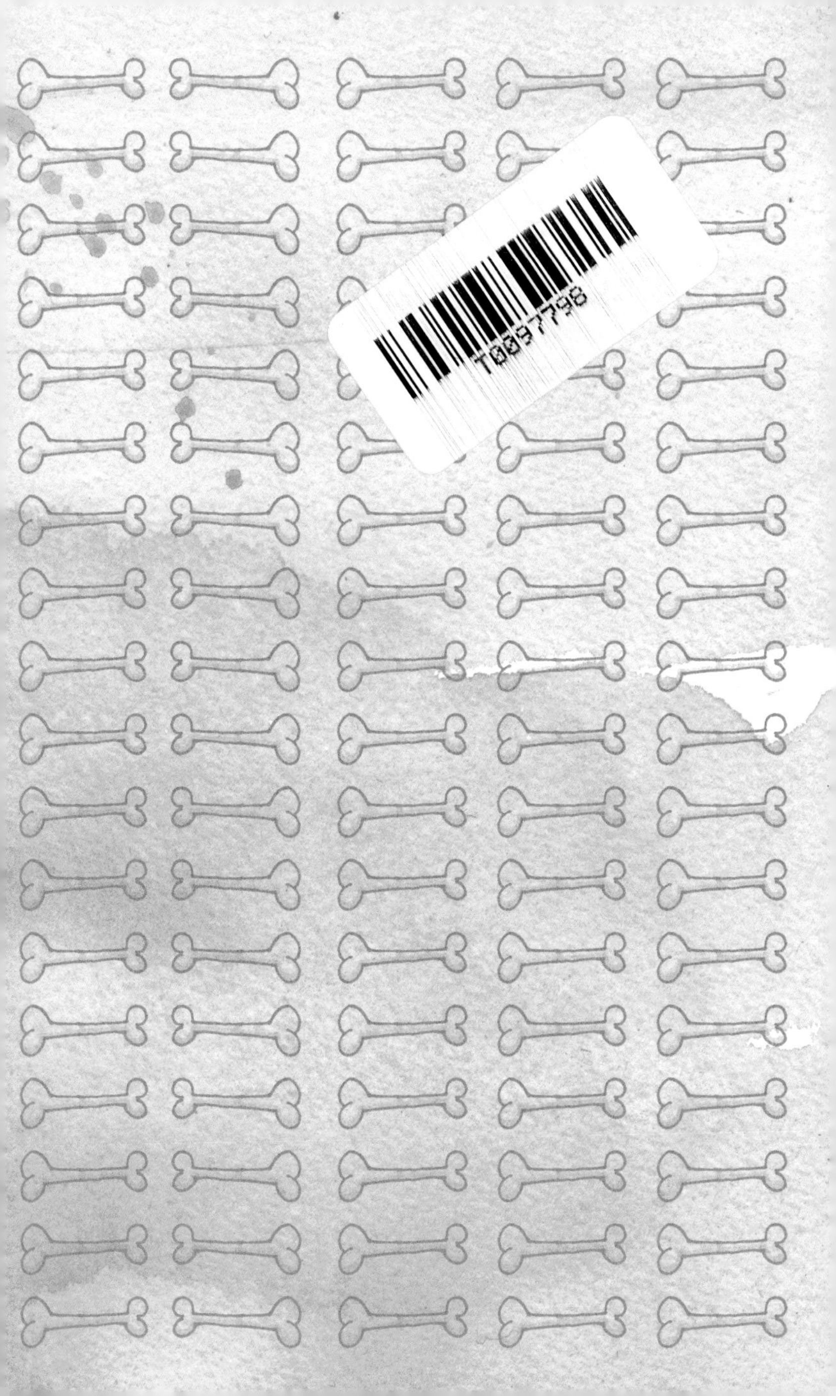

life lessons from a
DACHSHUND

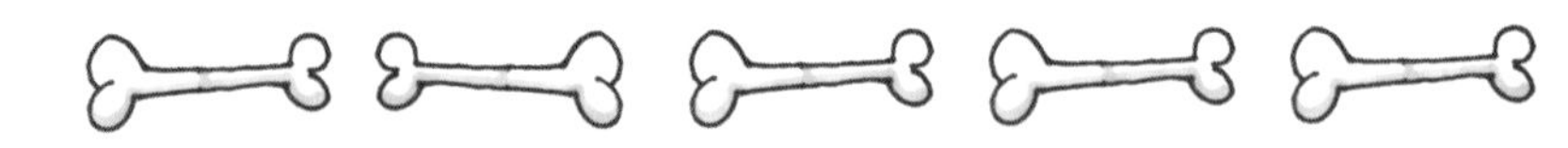

Published in 2020 by Dog 'n' Bone Books
An imprint of Ryland Peters & Small Ltd
20–21 Jockey's Fields
London WC1R 4BW
341 E 116th St
New York, NY 10029

www.rylandpeters.com

10 9 8 7 6 5 4 3 2 1

A CIP catalog record for this book is available from the Library of Congress and the British Library.

ISBN: 978 1 912983 29 2

Printed in China

Illustrator: Will Broome

Commissioning editor: Kate Burkett
Senior designer: Emily Breen
Art director: Sally Powell
Production controller: Mai-Ling Collyer
Publishing manager: Penny Craig
Publisher: Cindy Richards

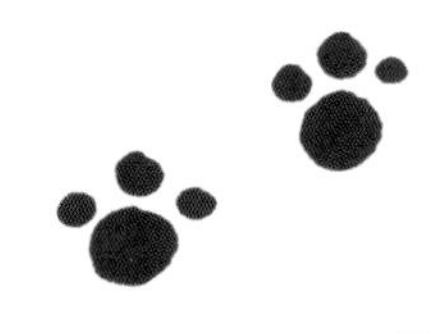

life lessons from a DACHSHUND

A DOG'S GUIDE TO LOVE, HAPPINESS, AND EVERYTHING IN BETWEEN

SIMON GLAZIN

illustrations by will broome

DOG 'n' BONE

CONTENTS

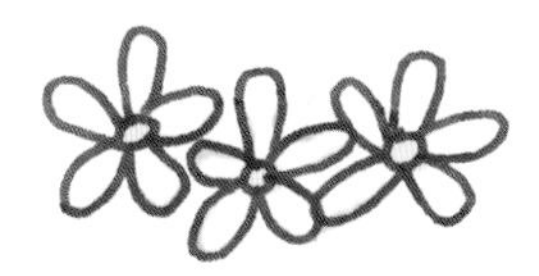

INTRODUCTION

Big things come in small packages: big personality, big bark, big puppy dog eyes, big appetite… the list goes on. OK, so we may not rank highly in the list of the cleverest dog breeds in the world, but we dachshunds are far from stupid. We know how to turn our small stature into big things. When we walk into a room, you notice us. When we bark, you pander to us. When we are determined to get something (food, toys, attention), you give it to us. When we don't want to do something, we stand our ground. And when the rain comes, we stay indoors.

We might have originally been bred to flush out badgers from their underground tunnels, but over the centuries we have developed many life skills to get us by in this big, modern world. For a dog that is approximately six inches tall, we can teach you humans a thing or two in order to win at life. For example, in a world where "throuples" are a thing, know that monogamy is still alive and well, and, when you've had a busy day, make sure to take time to self-reflect in a Zen space all of your own.

I'm Dhillon the daxie, and I'm here to guide you through all of the life lessons you can learn from us wiener dogs. So, take note and thank me later.

BIO

We dachshunds are obsessed with our owner(s), love food of any variety, aren't fussed about having any friends, but are confident, cute, and love nothing more than to curl up and sleep. I personally love tummy rubs, burying under the comforter, and getting an ear clean from my sister, Dolly.

AFFECTION (FOR OWNER):	**100**
AFFECTION (FOR OTHERS):	**2**
CONFIDENCE:	**76**
BARK LEVEL:	**89**
GUARD DOG:	**99**
CUTENESS:	**1,000,000**
TOP TRUMPS:	**WINNER**

DID YOU KNOW?

A dachshund was the first official mascot for the Olympics, created for the 1972 Summer Olympics in Munich, Germany. Designed by German designer Otto "Otl" Aicher, Waldi the wiener dog was chosen because of the breed's qualities; qualities that are also essential for an athlete: resistance, tenacity, and agility.

Dachshund means "badger dog" in German. No, we don't look like badgers, but we were originally trained to flush them—and smaller animals—out of their underground burrows. That's why we love digging so much!

We are the smallest hound breed. But, as they say, good things come in small packages.

Three wiener dogs are on the list of the world's oldest dogs on record, with a combined age of 61 years and 277 days.

We come in 15 colorways (from black and tan to red and wild boar), six marking types (brindle, dapple, double dapple, piebald, brindle piebald, and sable), three coat types (longhaired, shorthaired/smooth, and wirehaired), and two sizes (standard and miniature).

RELATIONSHIPS

LIFE LESSON: MONOGAMY IS ALIVE AND WELL

You thought love at first sight was saved for soppy, rom-com bonkbusters, but that couldn't be further from the truth. From the second a dachshund puppy lays eyes on its owner, that's it.

Cue heart eye emojis and cartoon cupid bow and arrows. We fall hook, line, and sinker. And just like Leonardo and Kate in *Titanic*, we can't take our eyes off each other. In fact, dachshunds won't settle unless we have one eye firmly on our owner, which may sound borderline controlling, but it comes from a place of feeling secure and safe.

Truly monogamous, dachshunds are one-owner only animals. The world may be leaning toward a much more relaxed view on relationships, but there's something to be said about sticking to one person. No open marriages or "throuples" (Google it!) here. Think of a dachshund/owner relationship similar to that of a couple who have been together for 60 plus years—you know full well that neither party has ever had their head turned. We dachshunds are jealous creatures—just one stroke of another dog and you'll know about it! If you're not after that all-encompassing, suffocating love, move on to another breed.

FAMOUS OWNERS AND THEIR DOGS

Thanks to some rather famous faces who have extraordinarily good taste, we daxies have fast become the dog breed *du jour*. Over the years, there have been lots of celebrities who have been avid dachshund lovers—it's nice to know we are in such good company.

ADELE AND LOUIE

Rumor Has It that the singer-songwriter and her pup are often found Chasing Pavements by the River Lea in London, UK, on their walks.

PABLO PICASSO AND LUMP

Adding "One of Picasso's muses" to your résumé is a highlight for anyone, especially little Lump, who also made an appearance in some of the artist's work.

ANDY WARHOL AND ARCHIE

Imagine the things Archie saw living with Andy. Imagine getting to sit on Edie Sedgwick's lap. We do hope this distinguished dachshund was a regular at Studio 54, too.

JOAN CRAWFORD AND STINKY AND PUPPCHEN

Joan loved her daxies, so much so that they often accompanied her on movie sets. But did they get their own trailer?

QUEEN VICTORIA AND BOY

The Royals have always loved dachshunds, and Queen Victoria was no exception with her beloved Boy. Queen Elizabeth loves the breed, too. Well, half the breed: she has dorgies—dachshund and corgi crosses.

DAVID HASSELHOFF AND HENRY

If you're awake early enough in Malibu, USA, you might spot David and Henry doing that famous run along the beach!

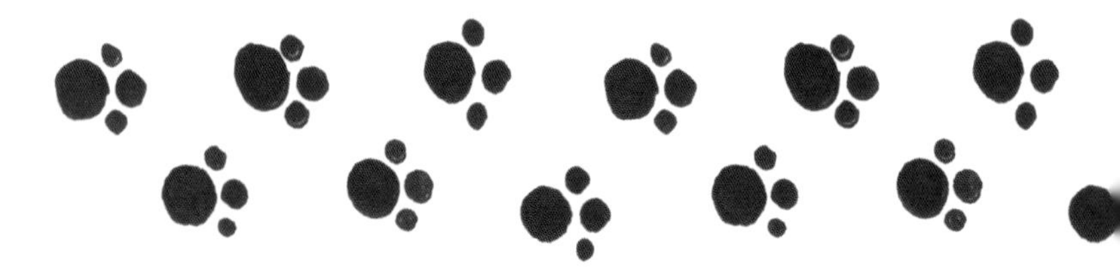

EMOTIONS

LIFE LESSON: DON'T BE SCARED TO SHOW YOUR FEELINGS

If there's one thing you will learn quickly, it's that dachshunds have emotions. All of them. And we're not afraid to show them. But don't let that scare you, we never show them all at once. In quick succession, maybe, but we won't bombard you. The minute you learn to harness them is the very moment you become a well-rounded ~~individual~~ dog.

LOVE

We've only got enough love for one person (two at a push): our owner(s). Everyone else we tolerate. We'll shower our owner(s) with love—unconditional, unwavering, full-on, heart eyes love—the kind of love that keeps you doing a little welcome home dance by the front door every single time. We also might poop on your pillow, but it's just one of the many ways we show our undying devotion to you—promise!

HATE

Just as you'll know for sure if a daxie loves you, you'll know pretty quickly if we dislike you or a situation. Side eye is a speciality of ours. Stroke us too much or not enough, leave us with someone we don't know, put us around little kids... all are triggers for that little beady eye to make an appearance. Come and say "hi" and sniff around, sure! But don't outstay your welcome—we've been known to bare some teeth.

JEALOUSY

As mentioned previously, daxies are the jealous type. Give so much as a glance at another pooch and you'll set us off. Attempt a stroke and you've crossed the line. Cue whining, pushing with our nose, or a terse bark to let you know that you've overstepped the mark. That dog is not worth your attention. I am. **ONLY ME**. Got it?

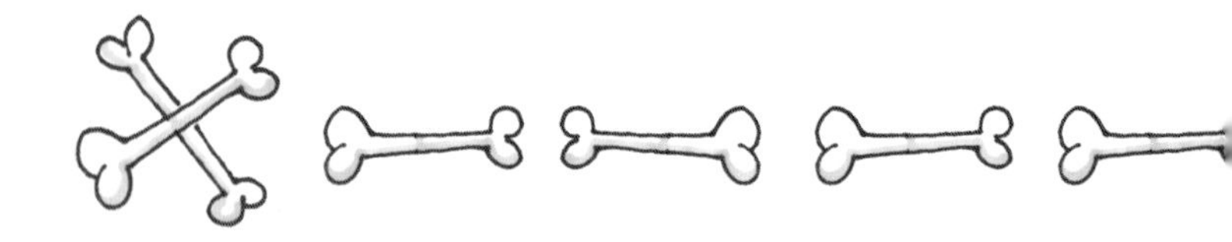

FEAR

Ever tried vacuuming around a wiener dog? We'll scarper in seconds. There's something about the noise and the suction, which makes us think the machines are about to gobble us up. (And don't think you've fooled us with those silent vacuums, we know exactly what their motive is!)

And those puppy dog eyes looking up at you when you leave the house? That's a paralyzing fear you're never coming back.

We dare not even mention the "v" word. We go full on tail-under-bum scared when we are dragged kicking and screaming to the vet. But you know what? In hindsight it's not that bad. Especially when they give us medicine that makes us feel like we're no longer going to throw up a kidney.

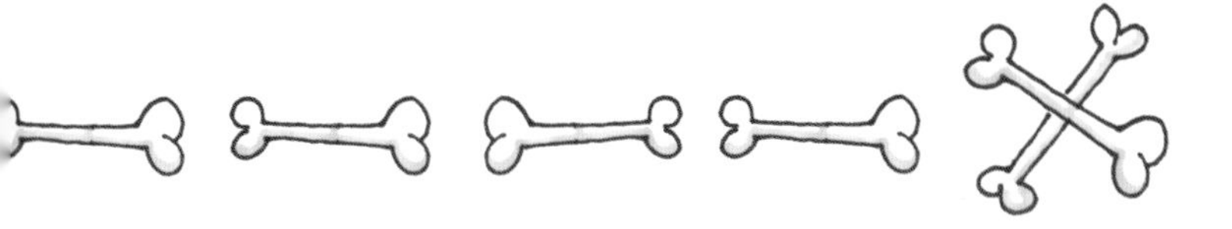

SOCIALIZING

LIFE LESSON: IT'S OK TO BE AN INTROVERT

Being one of the least sociable dog breeds of all time, get ready for a life of your owner constantly excusing your behavior. "Oh, ignore him, he barks at everyone!" or, "She'll only bite you if you get too close." Call us grumpy, we don't mind. By nature, we wiener dogs essentially only like our owner(s). That's not to say we don't have one good friend or someone to chase around the park, but if it was up to us, we'd happily sit on our master's lap forever and a day. Forget forcing friendships, it doesn't work on us. If, like us dachshunds, you're a true introvert, here are some lessons to live by.

- For an easy life, sniff or say "hi" to acquaintances. It's only polite. You don't have to make small talk. Just give a subtle nod of the head or a brief bark and walk on by. It's fine.
- If you don't make eye contact, no one can see you. Act like that overly friendly French bulldog is not there and maybe they'll just leave you the hell alone.
- If you do feel like socializing, limit yourself to a three-minute play date to show you're interested, then pretend to fall asleep. You'll fool everyone into thinking the excitement all got too much.
- If all else fails, growl and bare your teeth. They'll soon get the message that you're not one to be played with.

SOCIAL MEDIA

LIFE LESSON: DO IT FOR THE GRAM

If you haven't got your own Instagram account, do you even exist? We daxies are racking up more followers on social media than our owners (please tell me you're following @crusoe_dachshund? He's basically the king of us wiener dogs) and we're fast becoming the faces of—and ambassadors for—brands, endorsing products from dog food, dog beds, and dog collars to the odd security system. To increase your social media following, take note of these five simple rules...

strike a pose
vogue!

1 Dress up in something fabulous. People love to see a dachshund in the latest fashions.

2 Don't include your owner in your pics—no one's interested in seeing their face.

3 Get your human to take a "candid" snap of you asleep, teeth on show. These types of images seem to get all the likes.

4 Posting a **#TBT** picture of you as a puppy is a must. The cute factor will ensure thousands of likes.

5 Lastly, and most importantly, be strategic. Invite a friend who has a huge following to conduct a little photoshoot to post on your account. That way you'll get their followers liking and following you, too—genius!

So you can plan your content accordingly, here is the lowdown on which social media channels are which.

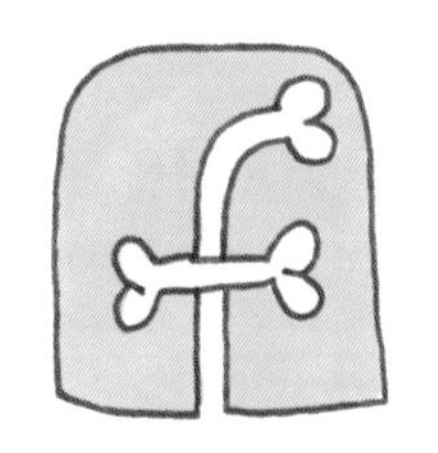

DOGBOOK

Use this platform to re-post fake news. Sharable content is king, and it's imperative your followers are made aware of the sick plot to hide sticks and chew toys worldwide.

PUPSTAGRAM

This is the channel to focus on picture postcard walkies. Post only the very best bits of your life on the gram—no one wants to see you crying into your kibble, double chin on show. Remember, if you don't get at least 20 percent of your audience liking every picture you post, you have failed. **OFF TO THE DOGHOUSE!**

WOOFER

Where once this was the channel for customer complaints, it's now the very spot where dog memes flourish. Turn your most embarrassing moments—clips of you falling down the stairs or running into a glass door—into gifs and post away. Just make sure you share in 280 characters or less, then sit back and watch the favorites and retweets rack up, and your followers increase.

DIGDOG

The aim of the game here is to make people howl. Mimic the latest dance craze or try the filter that superimposes your owner's lips onto your mouth and watch the reposts roll in.

FOOD

LIFE LESSON: BE (MODERATELY) ADVENTUROUS

Contrary to popular belief, we aren't like all the other breeds who will wolf anything down when it comes to dog food. We wiener dogs are actually quite fussy about our canine cuisine. We have been known to go on hunger strike if our human dares to give us different kibble than what we're used to.

When it comes to human food, however, we'll pretty much give anything a go. Lethal chocolate, a bite of chicken from your plate, or scraps of pizza going to waste on the street. There's no need for vacuuming when we're about (and that's not just because we're terrified of the things!). We'll make short work of anything that hits the floor.

A handy hint for you humans: don't turn your back on your plate for too long—our will power when it comes to resisting food is zero. We'll be up at the dining table before you can say, "Dhillon, don't!"

For future reference, some of our favorite foods include carrots, meat of any kind, peanut butter, and scrambled egg. Separate or all together in a Gordon Ramsay-worthy feast, either is fine by us. We might be small in stature, but that doesn't mean we can't eat our body weight in just about anything.

yum!
D

OBESITY EPIDEMIC!

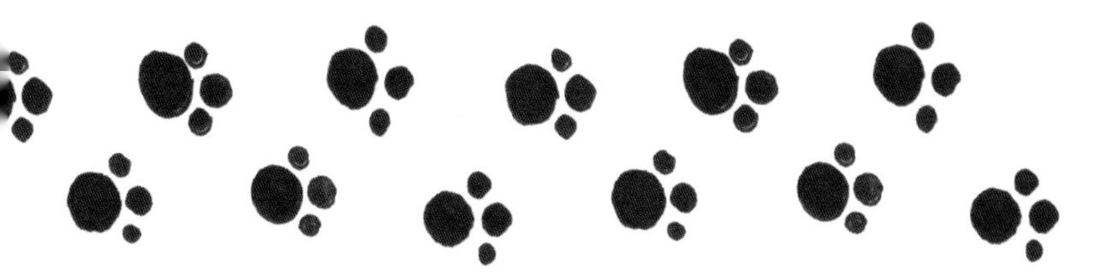

WEIGHT

The trouble with never feeling full is that you inevitably pile on the pounds. For a Great Dane, Labrador, or collie, a bit extra around the middle won't really matter—they have the height for it. But for us wiener dogs it's a different story.

You don't want to be the one that hits headlines because your stomach is touching the floor, you can no longer make it outside to relieve yourself, or you need to be cut out of your kennel. We're all for body positivity here—we'll paw pump any pooch who is happy in their own skin—but the simple fact is no one wants a diminutive dachshund that is about to explode.

And what's more, we have to take care of our joints, especially our long backs, which can be über sensitive if there's even a little bit of excess weight hanging about. So, do yourself a favor and eat in moderation, no matter what your stomach growls at you. When it comes to your appetite, it might be worth practicing the art of saying no.

EXERCISE

LIFE LESSON: KEEP MOVING

It's a common misconception to think that the smaller the dog, the less exercise we need. Having spoken about our love of food and ensuing weight issues, it must be said that we wiener dogs absolutely love to get our steps in. Humans think their recommended 10,000 steps a day is a lot, but left to our own devices, we'd happily double that (and suffer the consequences of joint pain afterwards.)

We even dream about exercising… Anyone else noticed our legs twitching when catching 40 winks? That's a sure sign of

our love of running, wind in our fur, through a field of grass just short enough so we can see, without a care in the world.

Weight training is not for us, mind you. You won't find us bench pressing 88lbs (40kgs) (and not just because our little legs can't lift much higher than our chests), but cardio... cardio we can do!

We do have to exercise caution, however. As with everything else in life, we daxies often think we can do more than we can and forget about our long spines that can often hinder our efforts. A piece of advice: exercise, yes, but don't overexert yourself—it's all about balance.

AT HOME

LIFE LESSON: FIND YOUR OWN SPACE

Mi casa es su casa, so says the daxie to its human. We wiener dogs really do like to make ourselves at home (so much so that we often believe you humans to be the house guest). Don't think for a moment the sofa will ever be just yours to sprawl out on. And if we're lucky enough to be allowed in your bed, you'll find yourself hanging onto the edge come morning. That, or we'll be proudly curled up on your pillow, sleeping right next to your head.

Having said that, we do love our own space away from everyone else. And there's only one way to truly be alone with your thoughts… by burying yourself in them under piles of dirty clothes, wet towels, the comforter. If there's somewhere we can burrow, we're happy. But watch out… there have been reports of humans scooping up the laundry and shoving it in the machine, not realizing one of us is in there.*

We also love to indulge in a bit of gardening. Digging is our forte—you've got our ancestral humans to thank for that—and we'll carry on flushing out the non-existent badgers while trying to reach middle earth until there's no garden left.

*I might have made that story up, but it could well happen!

Side note: *daxie owners beware. You'll soon develop an obsession with collecting anything that has a dachshund on it, be it a mug, candle, lamp, cushion, bedspread, or ornament. And even when you get to the point of never wanting to see another wiener dog-shaped plate again, you'll be gifted five for your birthday. Can you re-gift dog paraphernalia?*

GROOMING

LIFE LESSON: CELEBRATE SELF-CARE

We live in a time where self-care is very much the norm. Men use moisturizer or fake tan without being laughed at and women get blow dries on the daily. We daxies love to look good, too. Regular grooming is essential to keeping our coats looking glossy and healthy. Luckily, the smooth haired among us are pretty low maintenance, but we longhaired types often need some extra TLC—no one likes a knotted mane.

EARS

Give them a regular clean, or let your brother/sister/mum give them a lick. Ear infections are common among us daxies and they're hard to shake.

PAWS AND CLAWS

No one wants an ingrown nail, so be sure to book in for a pawdicure every so often. And keep those pads protected with some wax. It'll help in the cold, wet, or even hot weather.

TEETH

If there's one thing we hate having done, it's getting our teeth cleaned. Of course, we don't know the importance of dental hygiene, but we'll gladly lick the beef-flavored toothpaste all day long—delicious. If you don't brush often, be prepared to have those gnashers extracted.

PUBIC REGION

This one is specifically for the boys. Because we're low to the ground and the fact that some of us might be, erm, more blessed than others, we need to do some "manscaping" down there, just so nothing drags through the dirt, if you catch my drift.

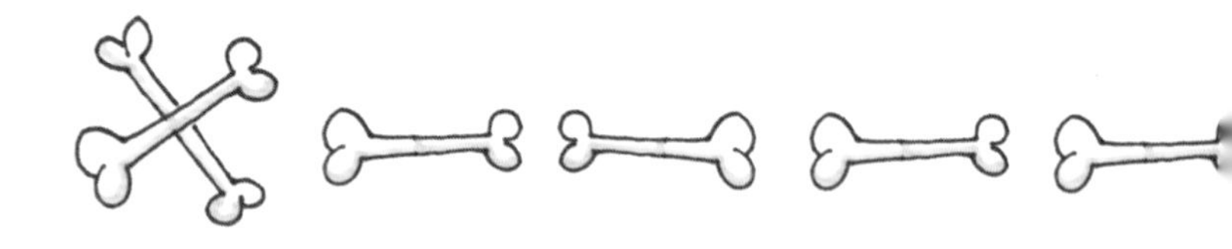

HAIRSTYLES

Just like you humans, we wiener dogs have hairstyles to suit every variety. Here's a little guide to the most requested dos in the doggy salon.

WIREHAIRED

The "styled to look shaggy" hipster do of the dachshund world. It's equally effortless as it is complicated—the beard to brow ratio is a fine line and can take you from looking like a grumpy old man to a super cute millennial.

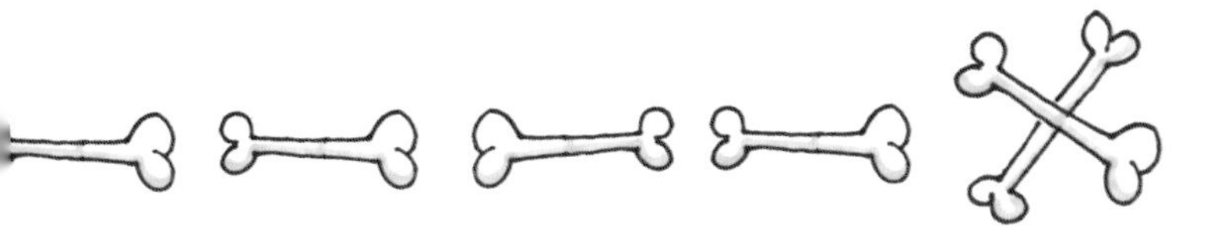

SMOOTH HAIRED

The perfect buzz cut for anyone who wants to wash and go, and not spend hours styling flyaways in front of the mirror. Humans pay good money for all kinds of serums and treatments to look as shiny as my **#BLESSED** smooth cousins.

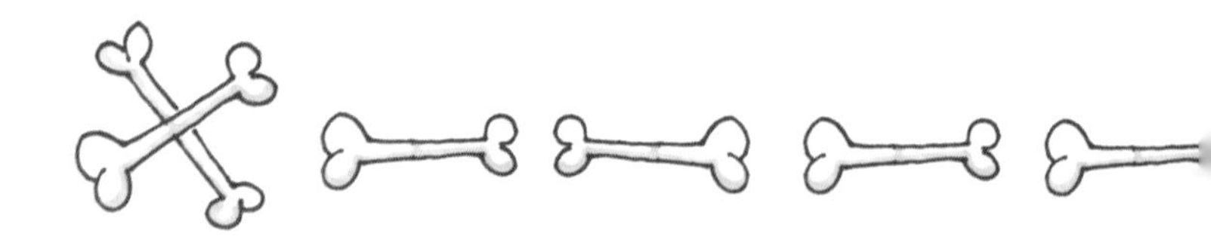

LONGHAIRED

A hairstyle trialed by many humans, but rarely executed well. It's hard to maintain to-the-floor hair and still look super chic, but somehow we manage it. And if you're lucky enough to live near the coast, just imagine that sea breeze running through your fur—how surfer chic!

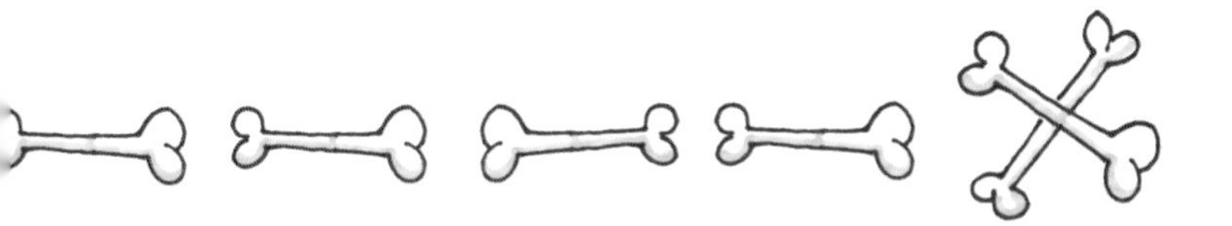

COLOR

Quite rare, but extremely eye-catching, dapple is a mottled, swirling, and spotty design. Try going into a salon and asking for this one!

Sable is essentially the equivalent of what humans like to call "balayage." Why they spend hundreds of dollars trying to look like they have roots when some of us are just naturally born that way is beyond me, but each to their own. Maybe we started the trend.

FASHION

LIFE LESSON: INVEST IN QUALITY COUTURE

As Vivienne Westwood once said, "Buy less. Choose well. Make it last. Quality, not quantity." Words to live by, both as dachshunds and humans. Owners love to dress their dogs up—not just dachshunds, but all breeds—and while there is lots of sartorial choice for our other four-legged friends, for us wiener dogs life is a little harder. Long bodies, small legs, protruding collar bones... all of these factors mean buying "off the peg" isn't conducive for fit or purpose. It seems couture is the only way forward for us pups.

Don't try and shove a daxie in a coat with long sleeves. Get us to walk and you'll soon see how hard it is for us to lift each leg. And would you go out in the bitter cold in a crop top? No, of course you wouldn't! So why should we? Think a "normal" dog jumper will suffice? Think again! It won't go far past our shoulder blades. Like you, we need something to cover our whole body. Just like shorter people, dachshunds' bodies are nearer the ground, so you also need to make sure nothing drags. A mohair covered in mud is never fun.

Getting our wardrobe right is a minefield. Maybe Westwood could create a canine capsule collection? Either way, brace yourself—and your credit card!

it's called fashion
look it up!

THE SENSES

LIFE LESSON: GO WITH YOUR GUT

SMELL

Dachshunds sniff everything and that's no exaggeration. We are, after all, part of the scent hound group. It's partly because we are so low to the ground and partly because we are one of the nosiest breeds ever, but on a walk, don't think you're going anywhere quickly. Our noses remain firmly pressed to the ground just so we don't miss a thing. We can even smell if our spaniel friend has been in the same spot two weeks prior, which shows just how refined our nostrils are. You might have misplaced our favorite toy, but leave it to Detective Dhillon to find it—I'll soon sniff it out.

SIGHT

We might be at ground level, but nothing gets past us. We see everything. Our sight is spot on from years of flushing out

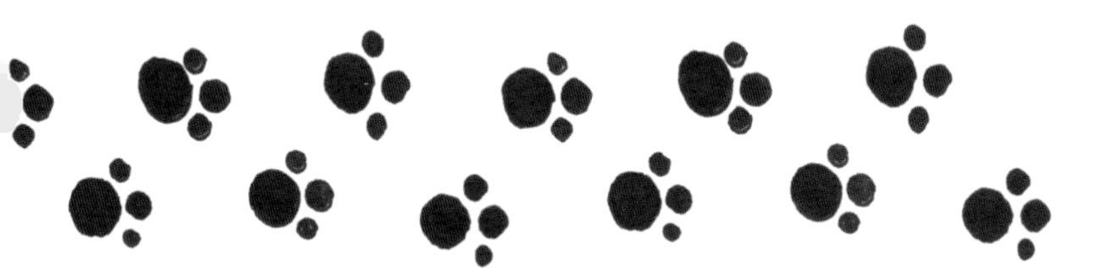

badgers from pitch black burrows. Let us off the leash at your peril: one glimmer of a squirrel's tail and we're off, trying to clamber up a tree to catch it. Not just a hunting device, we also use our eyes to lure you in, too—it's our way of getting attention. And believe me, it works! Puppy dog eyes have won me many a belly rub, more food, and a night in my owner's bed.

TASTE

Are your taste buds in need of some excitement? Then adopt our favorite food mantra: if in doubt, put it in your mouth. Nothing is off limits to us wiener dogs, even if it's potentially lethal. Hands up who has prized a piece of chocolate or a grape from our clamped jaws? We're adventurous to a fault: other dogs' poo, a three-course meal, ice cream—we'll eat anything. And don't think for a minute we'll ever be full. We'll eat our own food, then come and stare at you eating yours until you eventually give in and throw us some scraps.

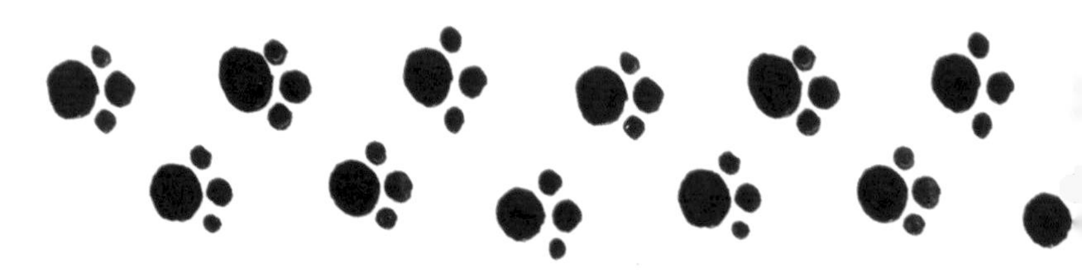

SOUND

Inbuilt supersonic hearing is another trait we have inherited from our ancestors. Our owners might think we don't know our own name when they're left screaming it at the top of their lungs, over and over again, but that's all a ploy—let's call it selective hearing. We have learned trigger words ("hungry," "walkies," and "wee wee"), and are skilled in recognizing our owner's car engine from two streets down, the postman's footsteps from three houses away, and the chinking of metal leash clips from somewhere in the house, which usually indicates an outing.

We also love a squeaky toy—the noisier the better. We consider that squeak a challenge and try desperately to beat our quickest time to destroy it.

TOUCH

As you'll see when it comes to the weather, we are very touch-sensitive. One drop of rain and the outside world is a no-go zone. And although we haven't quite perfected using our paws as you humans use your hands, you'll know all about it when we want attention… As well as working our magic with our big puppy dog eyes, we'll poke you with our noses over and over again until you cave and give us what we want.

CONFIDENCE

LIFE LESSON: WALK TALL

Dachshunds ooze confidence. Small is mighty. When we trot into a room full of people, we command it. Yes, it might be because we are extremely cute and immediately garner attention in the form of "oohs," "awws," and "aahs," but it's also due to the fact that we always have our heads held high—never in a pompous way, but just so people take notice.

The miniatures among us are not aware of just how mini we are—it's as though sometimes (read: all of the time) we consider ourselves big dogs. We'll quite happily approach a dog three times our size and bosh them on the nose to start a play fight, and we're also known to inject ourselves into groups of people having a picnic in the park in case there are some leftovers up for grabs. Shy, we are not.

When we are ganged up on by other mutts, we'll stand our ground and warn them off even though we might be petrified. We always endeavor to adopt the technique of walking tall, acting like we're in control and in charge, and displaying a confident attitude even when feeling vulnerable. The more we practice this skill, the more our confidence grows. It's all about faking it till you make it.

SUCCESS

LIFE LESSON: INCREASE YOUR APPETITE FOR SUCCESS

Whatever we dachshunds put our minds (and stomachs) to, we almost always succeed at. Some say stubbornness equals success and that's certainly true for us wiener dogs. We are as stubborn as an ox in everything we do, whether that be learning new tricks, toilet training, or choosing our route for walkies—the list is endless.

"No" is not in our vocabulary. If we come up against a challenge, we face it head on—sometimes literally (ramming something or someone out of the way is often the only way)! Follow these nuggets of wisdom to make a success out of everything in life.

• BE PERSISTENT. That squeak in your squeaky toy is there to be destroyed, and we'll keep going and going until we make it stop. And if that new ball gets wedged in between the couch cushions, we'll make it our life's mission to retrieve it.

• IT'S A DOG-EAT-DOG WORLD, SO SHARPEN YOUR CLAWS. This is particularly true when it comes to wiener dogs and our food. Drop something on the floor at your peril because we'll be right there to catch it. It's our "in the wild" conditioning kicking in—we've got to take what we can when we can for fear someone or something will take it away. That's why you'll often see us finishing the contents of a bowl of kibble in about two seconds flat.

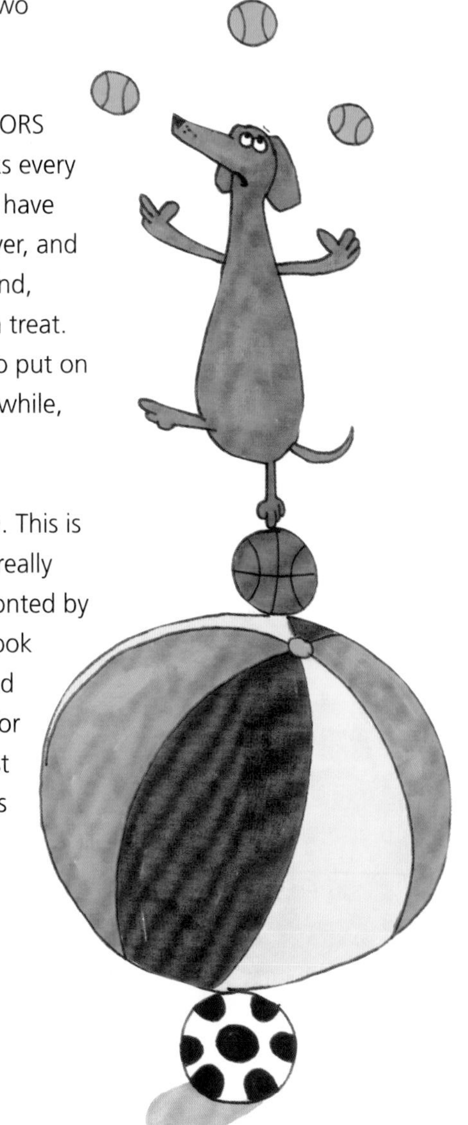

• INDULGE YOUR SUPERIORS by performing a few tricks every now and then. Once you have learned how to sit, roll over, and offer the paw on command, you'll be rewarded with a treat. It's in your own interest to put on a performance once in a while, trust me.

• STAND YOUR GROUND. This is where our stubbornness really comes in to play. If confronted by a dog we don't like the look of, one glance or bark and they usually retreat. But for those who are sent to test our patience, we'll give as good as we get and scream the loudest until the other is silenced.

TIME OUT

LIFE LESSON: MAKE TIME FOR "ME"

Who doesn't love some downtime? Those blissful few moments in the day where you've nothing to worry about but your own meandering thoughts—usually about food or running through a field. Or food.

It's important to make time for yourself, and they do say that silence is golden, right? But for us wiener dogs quiet time doesn't always mean we're reflecting on life. We could be chewing on that trainer, pair of glasses, or cushion that you left lying around again. Or maybe we've run off into the kitchen, jumped from the stool onto the table, and attacked the plate of piping hot chicken and vegetables you've left to rest while you accept your guests. What? It wasn't meant for us?

and breathe...

If you don't hear a peep from us, we've either taken ourselves off, flipped onto our backs, paws in the air, and caught up on some z's, or we're up to no good. Nine times out of ten, you can bet it's the latter.

BEING HEARD

LIFE LESSON: SPEAK UP FOR YOURSELF

Yes, we might like some quiet time every now and again, but nothing pleases us more than when we use our voice. Dachshunds should be seen and heard—so deep and loud is our voice that if you can't see us, you'd be forgiven for thinking it belongs to a Labrador or bullmastiff.

As puppies we're all cute and quiet, but as soon as we learn to speak up for ourselves, there's no shutting us up. Our mantra is: if in doubt, speak out. Wanting some attention? Ask for it. Hesitant about that stranger approaching? Shout loudly to warn others. On the sofa and want to get down? Whimper and whine until someone comes to rescue you. Lost something under the bed? Bark, bark, and bark again until your human retrieves it for you. You get the gist.

Humans have tried to rein in our barking for decades, but it just doesn't work. As you may well realize by now, we're stubborn creatures, and never more so than when it comes to being heard.

SAFEGUARDING

LIFE LESSON: PROTECT THE PEOPLE AND PLACES YOU LOVE

When on walks, we will protect our humans to the nth degree. Most people minding their own business will get an evil stare at the very least—often a growl, too. And as for other dogs… in our eyes they are all out to get us. **WE. MUST. PROTECT.** And barking is the only way we see fit. We'll raise the alarm and won't shut up until said dog is out of sight.

Different types of dachshund have different levels of safeguarding. The smooth haired among us tend to be extra cautious (by which I mean yappy)—strangers have no chance! Wirehaired wiener dogs will run up and down barking for a while, not knowing what to do with themselves, almost to expel pent up energy. And longhaired pups will take an interest before getting over it quite quickly.

When it comes to protecting property, we dachshunds are probably just as good, if not better, at guarding our humble abodes. (I'm not condoning the abandonment of alarm systems altogether—I'd hate to be the cause of thefts all around the world.) We come fitted with added extras, including:

IBARK

A sensor so sensitive that we can detect when somebody (usually the postman) is just considering stepping onto the driveway or pressing the doorbell. We'll bark and then bark some more until we know we and our humans are safe from harm—or until we're given a treat to keep our mouths busy.

WINDOW GUARD

If a window ledge is within reach, you'll find us sat on it, fending off any strangers who even so much as look at the house. A passerby who thinks we're being cute will get a shock if they tap on the window—cue Ferocious Mode.

STAND DOWN FEATURE

We'll act like we absolutely hate the strange person who has just rung the doorbell and gained entry to our home, no questions asked. That is until they crouch down to give us a stroke, at which point we'll run off scared to a corner of the room and stay there until they leave and the front door closes firmly behind them.

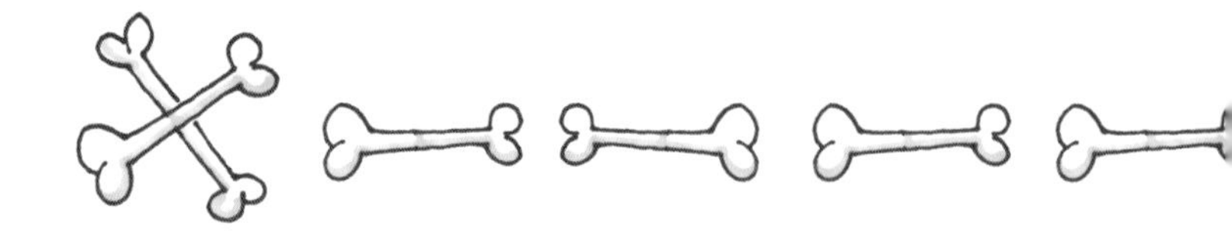

WEATHER

LIFE LESSON: IT'S OK TO LET THE WEATHER DICTATE YOUR MOOD

Unless you are a weather forecaster, talking about the elements has only ever been considered as filler conversation, small talk, or inane rhetoric that you spew when you don't have anything to say to whoever you are conversing with. But for us wiener dogs, it's probably one of the only things—apart from food—that actually dictates our mood and it's the line in the sand as to whether there will be any "walkies" or not (as you can imagine, the highlight of any dog's day).

It is proven that weather can affect one's emotional compass, so why not adopt a more daxie-like approach when it comes to climate?

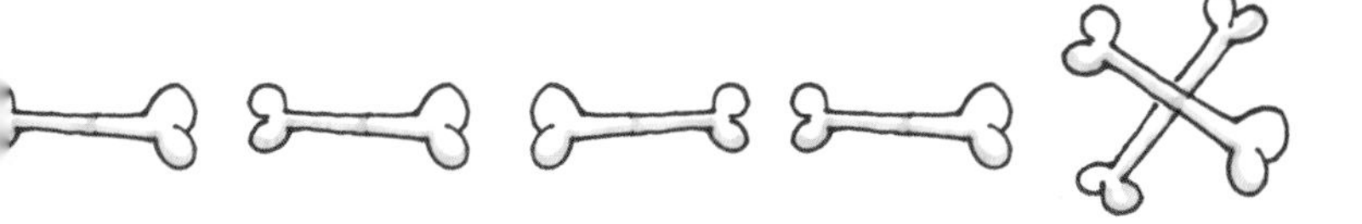

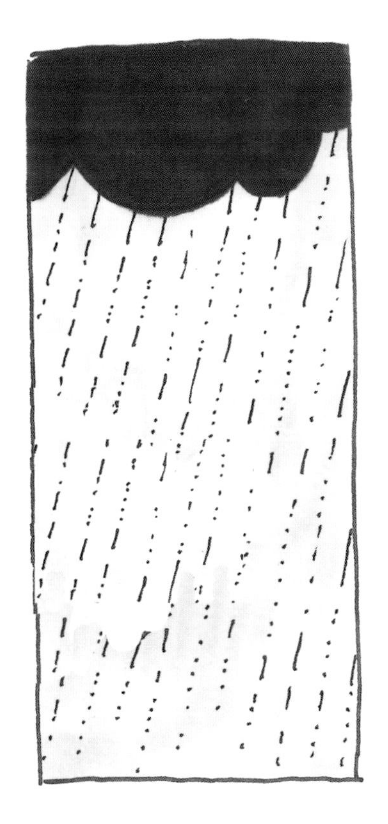

RAIN

Light, patchy, or heavy—it's immaterial what type of rain it is, we are categorically not going out in it. (I guarantee some of you humans are nodding your heads in acknowledgment of having to drag your dog around the block even in the lightest drizzle.) We have an inbuilt barometer that is so highly trained, we can smell the rain before it falls. The brakes go on before we have even left the house. Rain ruins hair, makeup, clothes, and moods. Take a leaf out of our book and call in sick when it pours.

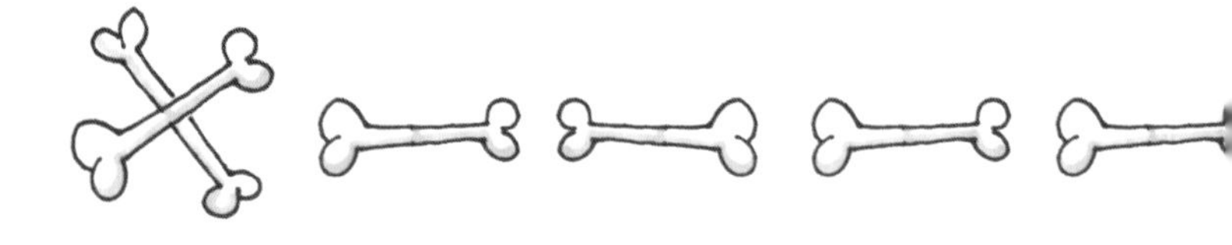

SNOW

It's all very fun for you watching us jump around in the snow, but for us all that bouncing is just an attempt to prevent the onset of frostbite. It might look picturesque, but really, it's an absolute nuisance. Go out in it by all means, make a snow angel, and build a snowdog, but make sure to wrap up warm and come inside the minute you feel like your paws might fall off.

HEAT

Although relatively OK in high temperatures, we would definitely prefer it to be spring all year round. Anything above 77°F (25°C) is cause for concern. We still enjoy walks, but make sure your human carries water with them—a dehydrated daxie will need rescuing quickly. And a brilliant tip: on scorching days, get your owner to touch the ground. If it's too hot for them, it's way too hot for daxie paws.

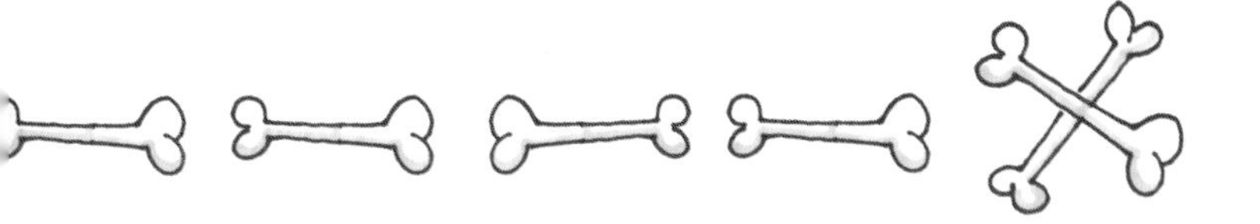

WIND

We might be sturdy creatures, but on days with strong winds humans run the risk of flying a dachshund kite, especially with the waif-like, smooth haired variety. Imagine long flapping ears like an unruly scarf—one blow in the wrong direction and you're in the dark. In gusty conditions, do your business in haste and get back inside to sort out your do.

ILLNESS

LIFE LESSON: LOOK AFTER YOURSELF

As dogs go, dachshunds are prone to illnesses ranging from dry heaving for attention, to physically throwing up because we decide that everything on a walk must be licked or eaten. If we could speak human, we would definitely be one of the only breeds to constantly moan of an ailment (until we take a doggy pain killer and then we're fine).

Our main affliction though is back injury. Having long, slender bodies supported by little legs means certain things should be adhered to. Namely, no climbing up and down stairs, no jumping on and off sofas and beds, and maintaining a healthy weight. Being the über stubborn creatures that we are though, we daxies will almost always try and get away with not doing any of the above. We're quite like you humans in that way, who, despite warnings against intense exercise, insist on lifting that 132lb (60kg) weight and end up slipping a disc. Please don't be that person. Look after yourself so you can look after us.

GETTING OLDER

LIFE LESSON: GROW OLD GRACEFULLY

Like any living mammal, age creeps up on us in many ways...

• WALKING BECOMES A CHORE. Whereas a younger daxie loves nothing more than chasing a ball through the grass, older wiener dogs are over fetch in approximately 12.5 minutes. And when we've had enough, you'll know all about it. We'll just sit there until you carry us home—what a treat!

• OUR FUR TURNS GRAY. It's only natural. Instead of masking the gray with highlights that cost a small fortune, we accept and embrace it. I have a friend whose once tan beard and eyebrows are now almost white—he's quite the silver fox!

• WE NEED WAY MORE SLEEP. Apparently, the 14 plus hours of shut eye we already get is not enough. We get tired a lot quicker—one lap around the park and we're done. But who doesn't love an additional 40 winks?

• WE NEED LOOKING AFTER THAT LITTLE BIT MORE. Our backs are pretty tenuous no matter our age, but us pups who are past our prime need extra care. Some of our humans invest in little ramps so we can negotiate getting up onto the sofa or into their bed. And you can forget about us climbing the stairs—from now on we need to be carried.

• THE WEATHER AFFECTS US SO MUCH MORE. The cold, wind, and rain are total no-nos—our joints ache and our paws are too precious for freezing, wet surfaces. The extreme heat can tire us out remarkably quickly, and snow is the enemy. If we could, we'd make it springtime all year round. Failing that, we tend to stay indoors in unsuitable weather.

SURVIVING IN A CITY

LIFE LESSON: ADAPT

We might have been bred to flush badgers out from the undergrowth, but centuries later we're much more at home on a busy commute or browsing the aisles of a store. That's not to say our time spent hunting hasn't taught us anything—those narrow burrows have allowed us modern types the ability to cope with small spaces. We can easily endure being crammed into our owner's handbag or being pressed up against sweaty people on the train. With plenty of experience in the area, here are my top tips for surviving in a city.

• KEEP YOURSELF TO YOURSELF. The less human/dog interaction you have, the better. This is easier said than done when you're a delightful and diminutive dachshund. Try not to snap when you're stroked or get your bum sniffed—a bit of side eye should be enough to get them to move on.

• PUT ON A SHOW. If your owner is single and walking you down a busy street, chances are they are looking to attract attention. Put on your best strut and really work it for them but remember to keep your wits about you and your jealousy in check—I've pooed on someone's shoe before because my human was being overly flirtatious. In hindsight, not a good look for anyone involved. And my owner never did get that date...

• MAKE YOURSELF AS SMALL AS POSSIBLE. This will allow you to dodge many an obstacle and get you to your destination twice as fast.

• ALWAYS DO YOUR BUSINESS IN DESIGNATED AREAS, not just in the middle of a busy sidewalk. It's not only embarrassing for you (some tourist will have their camera ready, mark my words), but equally as mortifying for your owner, especially if they are out of poop bags.

• BE FRIENDLY TO OTHER PUPS out on the streets or in city parks, as much as it irks you. This might not be familiar territory for them, and your help could very much make their day.

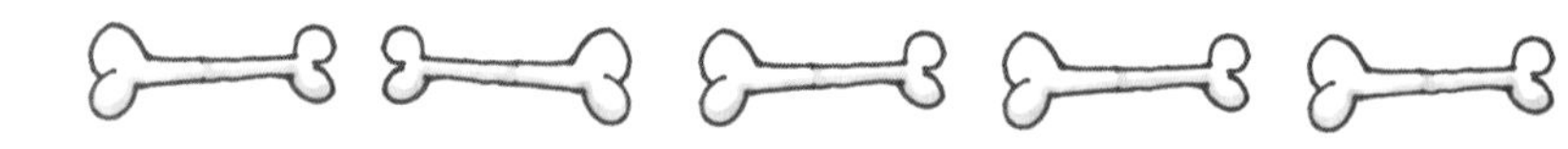

ACKNOWLEDGMENTS

I'd like to dedicate this book to my entire family—who are all dachshund obsessed and own wiener dogs in London, Worthing, and New York—and to everyone who has decided to give these perfect dogs a loving home around the world.

A special mention to my two absolutely incredible pups, Dhillon and Dolly. Without them, my life wouldn't be complete.

Simon.

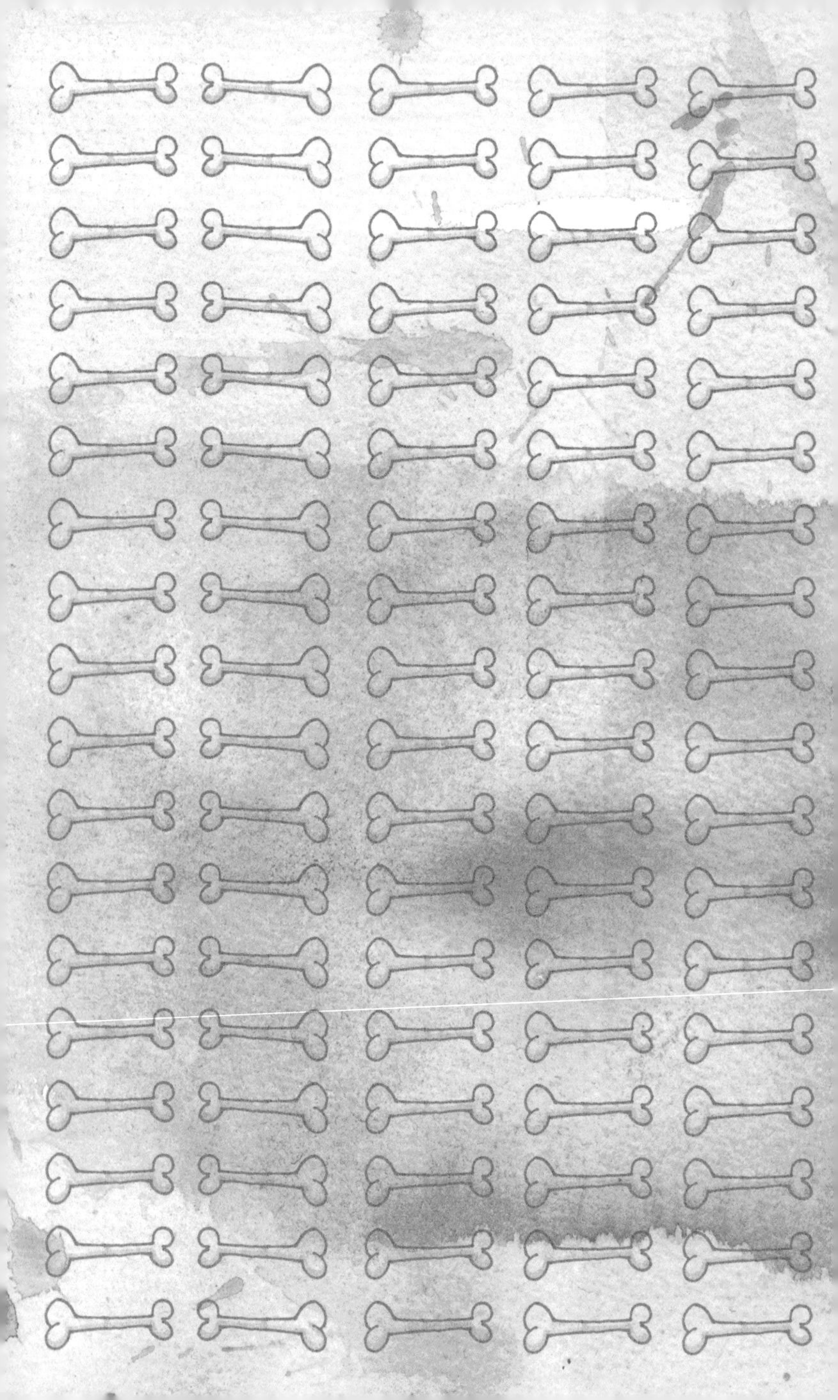